For Tanveen, Kiyaan and Zarann

"For god shows no partiality" Romans 2:11, Holy Bible: English Standard Version.

*"I am the same to all beings. I favour none, and I hate none.
But those who worship Me devotedly, they live in Me, and I in them." Verse 09.25, Bhagavad Gita.*

*"Someone is Hindu and someone a Muslim, then someone is Shia, and someone a Sunni,
but all the human beings, as a species, are recognized as one and the same."
Verse 85-15-1, Guru Gobind Singh, Akal Ustat, Guru Granth Sahib.*

*"We created You from a single (pair) Of a male and a female,
And made you into Nations and tribes, that Ye may know each other
(Not that ye may despise Each other)." Sūra 49: Hujurāt [Verse 13], The Noble Quran.*

*"and he denieth none that come to him, black and white, bond and free, male and female..."
2 Nephi 26:33, Book of Mormon.*

First published in 2020

Story & text by Kameel Vohra
Illustrations by Alvin Adhi Mulyono
Edited by Crystal Watanabe of Pikko's House

Visit our website at: **www.anikabooks.com**

Who's Inside that Hat?

This book belongs to :

....

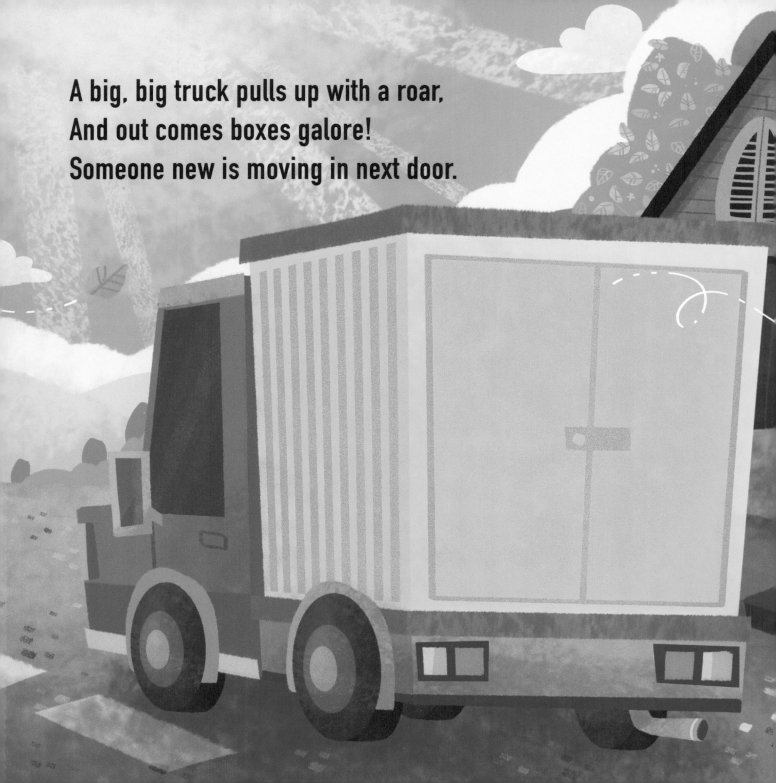

A big, big truck pulls up with a roar,
And out comes boxes galore!
Someone new is moving in next door.

"Who is moving in?" Anika asked, smile aglow.
She looked out through her bedroom window.
"Oh my! There's someone with a pointy black hat below!"

Anika peeked through the garden fence.
"There is something spooky that I sense!"
A big ugly wart on a nose so very intense.

Off down the road she goes, but wait, what's that?!
In her basket, she's got a black cat.
"Is she a witch? I need more facts!"

Following along, a safe distance behind.
She stops at a shop, and now she has a broom!
"Is she a witch?" Anika mused. "I do hope she's kind."

There's a gleam in her eye. She's seen something she likes.
Now she's buying vegetables and... Oh, yikes!

Oh no! Here she comes! Oh, what should Anika do?
"You're a witch," she cried, "you're going to make children stew!"
"Eat you?" said the witch. "I'm a vegetarian. That's definitely not true."

"You're a witch! You have a broomstick for flying at night."
"Ah, yes," said the witch. "My new broomstick, it's just the right height.
But don't be silly, it's not for taking a flight!"

"You're a witch," Anika cried. "I'm sure of it. You have a black cat!"
"Why, there's nothing wrong with that!
Would you rather I had a hairy pet bat?"

"You're a witch! I know it's true, you wear a pointy hat!"
"This? Yes, black hats are where it's at.
It keeps me cool and matches my cat."

"You're a witch! You have a scary wart."
The maybe-witch looked at Anika with a start.
"I got stung by a bee, and it sure does smart!"

"I'm Amelia, I'm not a witch, and I've got no magic spells, but I can bandage that knee in case it swells."

Anika thought and felt silly in the end.
"Thank you for helping. My scrape is on the mend,
and it's always nice to make a new friend."

How much do you remember from the story? Let's find out:

Remembering

Who are the main characters?

How many different creatures can you find in the story?

How would you describe Anika?

What did Anika think was scary about Amelia?

Understanding

Which part of the story did you like best? Why?

How do you think Amelia felt being called a "Witch"?

How would you have felt?

Why did Anika feel silly?

Applying

How could Anika have done things differently?

What is the moral of the story?

If you could change the ending, what would it be?

Who would you recommend this story to?

Can you draw your own comic version of the story?

Visit our website for lots of exciting
coloring sheets, puzzles and activities!

anikabooks.com/activities

CPSIA information can be obtained
at www.ICGtesting.com
Printed in the USA
BVHW022016070920
588264BV00012B/197